For my mother,
who taught me to see
what is beautiful, and
my father, who showed
me the joy of giving
GL

for Kirsty, with love
GH

LITTLE TIGER PRESS
An imprint of Magi Publications
I The Coda Centre, 189 Munster Road, London SW6 6AW
www.littletigerpress.com

First published in Great Britain 2003
This edition published 2004
Text copyright © Gillian Lobel 2003
Illustrations copyright © Gaby Hansen 2003
Gillian Lobel and Gaby Hansen have asserted their rights
to be identified as the author and illustrator of this work
under the Copyright, Designs and Patents Act, 1988.

A CIP catalogue record for this book is available
from the British Library

Printed in Singapore by Tien Wah Press Pte.
All rights reserved

ISBN 1 85430 896 3

4 6 8 10 9 7 5 3

LITTLE BEAR'S
SPECIAL
WISH

GILLIAN LOBEL

illustrated by

GABY HANSEN

Little Tiger Press
London

The sun was still in bed when
Little Brown Bear crept out into the shadowy woods.
"I wish, I wish . . ." he whispered.
"You're up early, Little Brown Bear!" called Lippity
Rabbit. "What are you wishing for?"
"It's my mummy's birthday," said Little Brown Bear,
"and I wish I could find the most special present
in all the world for her."
"I'll help you!" said Lippity Rabbit.
So off they went along the winding path. Little pools
of moonlight danced around their feet.

In the middle of the woods was a big rock.

Little Brown Bear sat down for a moment to think.

High above him glittered a star, so big and

bright he could almost touch it.

"I know – I could give my mummy a star,"

he said. "That would be a very special present."

Little Brown Bear gave
a little jump. But he
could not reach the star.

He gave a very big jump.
But still he could not reach
the star. Then Little Brown
Bear had an idea.

"I know!" he said. "If we climb to the very top of the hill, then we will be able to reach the stars!"

From the top of the hill the stars looked even brighter – and much nearer, too. Little Brown Bear stretched up on to his tiptoes. But the stars were still too far away. Then Little Brown Bear had a very good idea indeed.

"I know!" he said. "We must build
a big, big tower to the stars!"
"I'll help you!" said
Lippity Rabbit.

Together they piled the biggest stones they
could find, one on top of the other. Then they
stepped back and looked. A stone stairway
stretched to the stars.
"Now I shall reach a star for my mummy," said
Little Brown Bear happily. He climbed right to
the top and stretched out a paw.
But still he couldn't reach the stars.

"I know!" called Lippity Rabbit. "If I climb on your shoulders, then I can knock a star down with my long, loppy ears!"

Lippity Rabbit scrambled on to Little Brown Bear's shoulders. He stretched up his long, loppy ears. He waggled them furiously.

"Be careful, Lippity!" called Little Brown Bear. "You're making me wobble!"

Suddenly Little Brown Bear felt
something tapping his foot.
"Can I help you?" croaked
a voice.
"Why yes, Very Small Frog,"
said Little Brown Bear. "Are
you any good at jumping?"
Very Small Frog puffed
out his chest.
"Just watch me!" he said.
High into the air he flew,
and landed right
between Lippity
Rabbit's long,
loppy ears.

"Can you reach the brightest star from
there?" asked Little Brown Bear.
"No problem!" shouted Very Small Frog.
He took a mighty breath. "Look out,
stars, here I come!" he shouted.

Very Small Frog gave a great push with
his strong back legs. Up, up, up he sailed.
Lippity Rabbit's long, loppy ears twirled
round and round.

"Help!" he shouted. "Somebody save me!"

Backwards and forwards he swayed, and
backwards and forwards swayed Little Brown Bear.
With a mighty crash the stone tower toppled
to the ground. And down and down tumbled
Lippity Rabbit and Little Brown Bear.

"I can't breathe, Lippity!" gasped Little
  Brown Bear. "You're sitting right on by dose!"

Then Very Small Frog sailed down from the
stars and landed on Lippity Rabbit's head.
"I'm sorry, Little Brown Bear," he said. "I
  jumped right over the moon, but I still
  couldn't reach the stars."

Little Brown Bear sat up carefully.

His nose was scratched and his head hurt.

"Now my special wish will *never* come true,"
he said. "I shall never find a star for my mummy!"

"Don't be sad, Little Brown Bear," said Lippity Rabbit.

And he gave him a big hug.

A tear ran down Little Brown Bear's nose, and
splashed into a tiny pool at his feet.

As he rubbed his eyes, Little Brown Bear
saw something that danced and sparkled in
the shining water. Surely it was his star!
Little Brown Bear jumped up with excitement.
"Now I know what to do!" he cried.

Off he ran down the hillside.
"Wait for us!" cried Lippity Rabbit
and Very Small Frog.

Through the ferny woods they ran, over the silver meadows, until they reached the stream. For a long time they hunted along the sandy shore until Little Brown Bear found just what he was looking for. Then carefully, carefully, he carried it all the way home.

"Happy birthday, Mummy!" he cried.

Into his mother's lap he placed a pearly shell that shone like a rainbow. There, in the heart of the shell, a tiny pool of water quivered. And in that pool a very special star shimmered and shook – the star that had made a little bear's birthday wish come true.

"Lippity Rabbit and Very Small Frog helped me find the shell, but I caught the star all by myself!" said Little Brown Bear proudly.

Mother Bear knelt down and gave him a big hug. "Thank you all very much," she said. "This is a very special birthday present indeed!"

Make every day special with books from Little Tiger Press

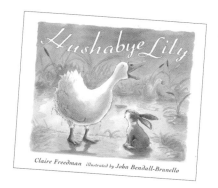

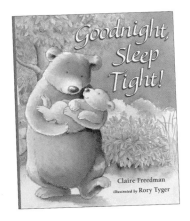

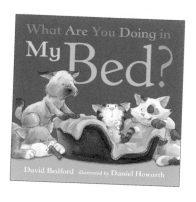

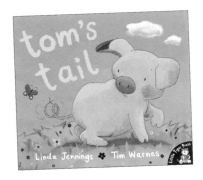

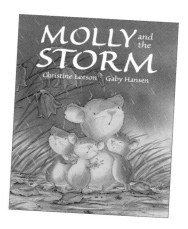

For information regarding any of the above
titles or for our catalogue, please contact us:
Little Tiger Press, 1 The Coda Centre,
189 Munster Road, London SW6 6AW, UK
Tel: 020 7385 6333 · Fax: 020 7385 7333
e-mail: info@littletiger.co.uk
www.littletigerpress.com